JAMIE AND ANGUS FOREVER

Anne Fine

Illustrated by Penny Dale

First published in Great Britain
in 2009
by Walker Books Ltd
This Large Print edition published
2010 by BBC Audiobooks Ltd
by arrangement with
Walker Books Ltd

ISBN: 978 1405 663649

British Library Cataloguing in Publication Data available

Printed and bound in Great Britain by
CPI Antony Rowe, Chippenham and Eastbourne

For Zachary Boynton Fine
A. F.

For Zachary Owen Horner
P. D.

CONTENTS

PLAYING AT BEING FRIENDS

Jamie and Angus were at the table. Jamie was finishing his toast and Angus was watching. Mummy was reading the paper and Daddy was stirring his third cup of tea.

"Saturday!" said Daddy. "Good old Saturday!" He turned to Jamie. "So tell me, what are you and Angus going to do this morning?"

Jamie looked at Angus. He looked at his four tiny hooves and his two bumpy horns and his round little snout and his big, hopeful, friendly eyes.

"Today," said Jamie, "Angus and I are going to pretend to be friends."

Mummy peered over the paper. "Pretend to be friends?" she said, smiling. "But you two do almost everything together. You know everything about each other's lives. And you hardly ever get fed up with one another. So you are friends already."

"Maybe," said Jamie. "Maybe we are friends already. But that's still what we're going to do today—pretend to be friends."

"Fair enough," Mummy said, and she went back to reading the paper.

Jamie picked Angus up off the table and carried him to the back door. He put him on the step outside, next to the tub

of flowers. "You wait here," he told Angus. "I won't be very long."

Angus stood waiting while Jamie closed the door and went back to his place at the table.

"If it's all right with you," he told his mother and father, "I have a friend coming over to play today."

"Oh, yes?" said Jamie's father. "And who would that be?"

"His name is Angus," Jamie said. "We get on well and I think we could be really good friends."

"That's nice," said Daddy. "When is this Angus coming?"

"Soon," Jamie told him. "Very soon. In fact, I rather think he might be here already."

"Is that right?" said Mummy.

"Yes," Jamie said. "In fact I think he might be waiting outside."

"Invite him in, then!" Daddy said. "Don't leave

5

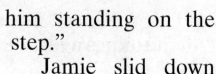

him standing on the step."

Jamie slid down from his place at the table and opened the door. Angus was looking at him hopefully.

"Ah!" Jamie said, delighted. "You're here!"

He carried Angus inside and held him up so Daddy and Mummy could see him properly.

"This is my friend Angus," he explained. "He's a little Highland bull."

"We're very pleased to meet you," Mummy said to Angus.

"We've heard a lot about you," Daddy said.

Angus looked slightly embarrassed.

6

"Don't worry," Daddy added hastily. "All the things we've heard about you are *nice* things."

"That's because Angus is my *friend*," Jamie explained. He tucked Angus firmly under his arm and told his parents, "We're going out into the garden now."

"Righty-ho," Daddy said. "Come back inside if you need anything."

"Righty-ho," Jamie echoed.

And off they went, Jamie and Angus, into the garden to play at being friends.

Jamie sat on the swing. "Do you like swinging?" he asked Angus politely.

Angus looked rather as if he did, so Jamie put him on his knee and they had a good long swing together.

7

"Do you like balancing along the edge of the flower beds?" Jamie asked after a while.

It seemed that Angus did, so off they went to do that next.

"What about football?" asked Jamie when they had reached the end of the last flower bed. But Angus wasn't very good at that. Every time

8

Jamie kicked the ball to him, he couldn't help falling over.

"It doesn't matter," Jamie comforted him. "We'll just do something else."

They built a secret place. Jamie took Angus into the house to show him the things they needed. The battered box was in Jamie's bedroom. So was the torn sheet, and the grubby old bath mat

Mummy had wanted to put in the rubbish bin. After he'd dropped the bath mat and sheet into the box, Jamie showed Angus around his bedroom.

"Maybe we'll play in here after lunch," he said. "Or if it rains."

Jamie carried the battered box into the garden and laid it on its side. He put the grubby old bath mat flat on the bottom to make the ground more comfy, and draped the torn sheet over the top.

"There," he told Angus proudly. "Our own little secret place."

Jamie and Angus spent a long time sitting together contentedly in the box. Jamie told Angus all about himself, and put his head down low so he could hear if Angus wanted to tell him anything back.

Halfway through the morning, they heard someone coming.

Jamie peeped out. Daddy was standing on the lawn holding a plastic plate on which were slices of apple and orange, two halves of banana and a small bowl of raisins.

"Oh, dear!" Jamie's father was saying. "I've brought this snack outside for

Jamie and his charming new friend, Angus. But it seems they've gone off somewhere secret."

He put the plate down on the grass. "I'll leave it here," he said. "In case they come back and feel a little peckish."

Between them, Jamie and Angus ate most of the snack. Then they thought up more things to do together. They leaned over the fence to say hello to Mrs Beadle next door. They made sand puddings in the messy corner of the garden. They picked some daisies and tied them into a posy with a long bendy grass stalk. (Jamie did the knot.)

Then it started to rain.

Jamie packed up the secret place. He folded the bath mat and put the sheet inside the box, stamped on the sand puddings, then carried the box indoors. After that, he went back for the daisies.

Jamie handed the posy of little flowers to his mother. "These are for you and Daddy," he said. "They are

from Angus. He wants to thank you for having him. He's had a lovely time."

"I'm glad," said Mummy. "And I'm delighted that you have such a sweet and good-mannered friend."

"I thought you would be," Jamie said.

"What are you doing now?" asked Daddy.

Jamie shrugged. "That game's all over," he told them. "We've stopped pretending to be friends. Angus and I are going to do other things."

And off they went, to do more things together. Jamie and Angus. Not pretending any more.

Just friends.

THE FEELING-BETTER SPELLS

Jamie came out of nursery and told his granny, who had come to pick him up, "Well, that was a horrible, no-good, absolutely terrible everything-go-wrong day!"

16

"Really?" said Granny.

"Really!" insisted Jamie. "First, I spilled milk from my cereal all over Angus's front hooves."

"Oh dear," said Granny. "Spilled milk is tricky, and his hooves might dry off smelly."

"He didn't look pleased," admitted Jamie. "And then I had to rush to get ready for nursery when I thought it was a lazy old staying-at-home day."

"It's always a bit of a bother getting you off to nursery," said Granny. "But you usually enjoy it once you're there."

"I might have," Jamie admitted. "If only I could have found my red trousers so I could show everyone the dragon on the patch at the back."

17

Granny shook her head. "Annoying. Perhaps they were still in the wash."

"Probably." Jamie shrugged. "Except that they wouldn't have helped very much because I'm the only one who didn't get a go on the new scooty tortoise."

"Why not?" asked Granny.

Jamie scowled. "Because, just before it was my turn, one of the wheels fell off."

"What rotten luck," said Granny. "I certainly hope that was the end of your troubles."

"Well, it wasn't," Jamie grumbled. "Because with our snack we had the wrong sort of cheese."

"You *hate* the wrong sort of cheese. I know that," Granny sympathized.

"And then Maria hit me. And Anthony laughed."

"Worse and *worse*," murmured Granny.

"Yes," Jamie said. He liked the sound of that, so he said it too, but much, much louder. "Worse and *worse*! And then a fire engine went past, and by the time I found a place on the fence where I could get my shoe to stick so I could pull myself up like everyone else and see it properly, it had gone round the corner."

"That's *terrible*," said Granny. "Can there be anything else after all that?"

"Just one more thing," said Jamie. "I didn't know I would be coming to your house till Mummy and I were nearly at nursery. So I didn't bring Angus to leave on the Safe Shelf till you came to pick me up."

19

He gave Granny a shy little sideways peep. He didn't want to be rude, but what he was going to say last was still the truth. "So now I've got to be at your house without him, and I won't get to see him till bedtime."

"Well," Granny said. "That certainly was a horrible, no-good, absolutely terrible everything-go-wrong day."

After tea, Granny asked Jamie, "What do you feel like doing, sweetie-pie?"

Jamie considered. "Well," he said. "I might be your sweetie-pie, but inside I'm still very cross. So I'd quite like to *bash* something. Really hard."

"Bashing something would make you feel better?" Granny asked.

"Yes," Jamie said. "I really think that bashing something really hard would make me feel better."

"Right, then," his granny told him. "I have just the thing."

She went to the big cupboard and took a smart green plastic

tub out from where it was hidden, right at the back. It was a clay bin, just like the one at nursery, but smaller.

Granny put it on the table. "I was keeping this for your birthday," she told Jamie. "But now I think that maybe you need it a whole lot more today."

Jamie prised off the lid. Inside was a big lump of clay, some cutters just like the ones they used at nursery when they were pretending to make jam tarts, and a set of wooden paddles. Some of the paddles had patterns on both sides so you could press them into the shapes you cut out to make them look more fancy.

Jamie was thrilled. When he had thanked Granny and given her a big hug, he helped her spread   a

plastic sheet over the table and settled down to making himself feel better.

First he pulled a little lump off the big lump in the clay bin, and then he bashed it.

Hard.

Bash, bash!

"That's for the milk spilling all over Angus's hooves and probably ending up *smelly*," he said crossly.

He bashed and bashed, until the clay lump was quite flat.

He prised off another lump.

Bash, bash!

"And that's for having to rush to get ready for nursery when I thought it was going to be a lazy old staying-at-home day."

23

He bashed a third lump.
Bash, bash, bash, bash!
"That's for not being able to find my red trousers with the dragon patch."

He pulled off a really big lump next, and bashed it as hard as he could with two of the little wooden paddles.

"And that's for not getting a turn on the scooty tortoise!"

He turned to Granny. "I'm only going to bash a small lump for the wrong sort of cheese," he explained, "because I wasn't really hungry anyway. But it's going to be big lumps for Maria hitting me and Anthony laughing, and missing the fire engine."

"What about forgetting Angus?" asked Granny. "Big lump or small for that?"

"Medium," admitted Jamie. "Because I'm really enjoying myself sitting here bashing this clay, and it's only till bedtime anyway."

Jamie kept

25

bashing his clay lumps until they were thin and flat and his arms and fists were tired. Then he set out the shape cutters in a row to choose between the square, the circle, the moon and the star. He chose the circle. He pressed it down on each of the flattened lumps in turn, and tore away all the untidy clay spread outside the edges. He pounded all that into one big lump again, and threw it back in the clay bin, out of the way.

Then he used all the different patterns on the paddles to make his beautiful circles more interesting on top.

Granny came up behind him. "They look splendid," she told him admiringly. "Like all those old pills Grandpa used to have, but a lot bigger."

"They're *spells*," Jamie explained. "They're all my feeling-better spells." He pointed to each in turn. "This one's my find-my-red-trousers-next-time spell, and this one's my don't-spill-milk spell. This is my not-having-to-rush spell, and this is my wheel-won't fall-off-the-scooty-tortoise spell."

"Let me guess," Granny interrupted him. "This one's the no-more-wrong-sort-of-cheese spell, and these two are the Maria-had-better-not-hit and Anthony-had-better-not-laugh spells."

Jamie pointed at the last of the little clay circles. "And this is the see-the-fire-engine-next-time spell and the don't-forget-Angus spell." He waved his hand over all of them. "And they're a lot bigger than Grandpa's pills ever used to be because they *work* better."

He and Granny were quiet for just a little while, thinking about Grandpa. Then Jamie scooped up his fancy clay spells and mashed them together in one big lump.

"You didn't bother to keep those long, did you?" Granny said.

Jamie put all the clay back in the bin and jammed the lid on firmly. "That's because I don't need them any more," he explained to Granny. "They've already worked, and I feel a whole lot better after my horrible, no-good, absolutely terrible everything-go-wrong day."

"That's splendid," said Granny, looking at her watch. "Because it's time to go home now, to see Mummy and Daddy."

"And Angus," Jamie reminded her.

"Oh, yes," said Granny. "Mustn't forget *him*. And Angus."

And she went off to find the car keys while Jamie put the clay bin away where it came from, hidden at the back of the cupboard.

A WHOLE *YEAR*

Jamie was jumping up and down on the rug, waiting for his birthday.

"A whole year!" he kept saying. "A whole *year*! Why do we have to wait a whole year between birthdays? It's far too long."

He turned to Angus. "It's twelve whole months," he told the little Highland bull, and started jumping them out on the rug. "January, February, March, April, May…" He wasn't sure if it was June or July that came after May, so he stopped leaping up and down.

"I'm a bit puffed now," he explained, and went over to take one more look at the birthday cake that his mother and father were finishing. It had been made to look like a big bouncy castle. Mummy had cooked all the puffy pink sponge bits and, now they were cool, Daddy was sticking them together with fudge icing. Before all his friends arrived for tomorrow's party, Jamie was going to choose a few of the tiny plastic animals at the bottom of his toy box and scrub them clean, then stick them on top to look as if they were bouncing.

"A whole *year*," he complained again. "That's twelve whole months since I last had a birthday."

Suddenly Jamie noticed that Angus wasn't looking at the cake. He was gazing into the distance, as if he was thinking.

He didn't look as if he was thinking happy thoughts.

Jamie stopped hugging himself and picked up Angus to hug him instead.

"Should Angus have a birthday too?" he asked his mother. "I know he was just sewn together and not really *born*. But it still *happened*, didn't it? So surely he should get one as well."

"But we don't know how long he'd been in the shop before we bought him," Mummy reminded Jamie. "So we don't know which day is his birthday."

Jamie hugged Angus closer. "He can have the same one as me, then," he said. "If Angus doesn't have a birthday of his own, he can share mine."

And since the cake

was huge (and Angus didn't eat cake anyway) he added generously, "And we'll start tomorrow."

Next day, at teatime, Jamie's friends from nursery came to his party. Tasha was there. And Arif. And Max and Georgie. Bella came with her mother. Nana came. Flora the babysitter even popped in for a while. And Granny rang from Spain where she was on holiday.

"I'm sharing everything with Angus today," Jamie announced. "My birthday and the party. Everything."

They had a wonderful time. They ran races round the garden. They played musical games. They played pin the tail on the donkey. (Bella won that because she was shaking her head about so much her blindfold slipped, but nobody minded.)

Then they had the birthday tea. Daddy took photos of the

cake before Jamie prised off the little plastic animals and sucked the icing off their hooves and paws so he could put them back in the toy box.

While everyone was busy eating cake, the doorbell rang. Jamie slid off his chair. He picked up Angus (because he was sharing everything with him today) and ran to the door.

Uncle Edward was standing there holding a big box wrapped in bright paper. "I can't stay," he said. "I'm still at work. But I was driving past your house so I stopped by to give you this. Happy birthday!" He handed the present to Jamie.

"I'll have to open it with Angus," Jamie warned him. "Because we're sharing everything today—even my birthday."

"Jolly good," said Uncle Edward, and he bent down to kiss Angus firmly on the snout. "Happy birthday to you too, then, Angus."

Jamie shook the box. It rattled quite a bit. "Have you given me another of what Daddy calls your really impossible presents?" he asked his uncle. "Like the false beard I kept tripping over. And the clockwork rat that nearly gave Granny a heart attack."

Uncle Edward grinned. "Oh, yes," he said. "I think I can honestly say that this is one of my really impossible presents."

And he hurried off, to be safely away before Jamie's mother or father could scold him for buying another of his really impossible presents for Jamie.

Jamie and Angus rushed back to the party. While everyone watched, Jamie tore at the wrappings. He helped Angus use one of his hooves to pull off a bit of the paper because they were sharing everything. Then he opened the box.

Inside were dozens and dozens of party streamers.

"Brilliant!" said Jamie. "I *love* party streamers. I love pulling the string until

they go *pop*! I love the way the great long threads of coloured paper shoot out and tangle over everything."

He dipped both hands in the box and stirred the tiny tubs of party streamers round and round. "There are *hundreds*!" he said excitedly. "There are enough for everyone to have handfuls and handfuls, and then some more."

"Oh, brilliant!" Jamie's father rolled his eyes. "And what a tremendous shame that Uncle Edward couldn't stay long enough to help us clear up all the mess afterwards."

Jamie tipped all the party streamers out onto the floor.

"You don't have to pop the whole lot today," Mummy said hopefully.

"I do," insisted Jamie. "Because party streamers are perfect for birthdays, and it will be twelve whole months before Angus and I get to have another. That's a *whole year*."

Jamie made all his friends stand in a circle. He poured a little heap of party streamers in front of each of them. Then, while he was still in the middle, making sure everyone's pile was exactly the same size, Arif had an idea.

"The streamers were Jamie's present," he told everybody. "So we should use them to decorate Jamie." He picked up the first of his streamers and pointed it at the ceiling. Then he pulled the string.

Pop! went the tiny tub, and the lovely threads of coloured paper shot up to the ceiling and

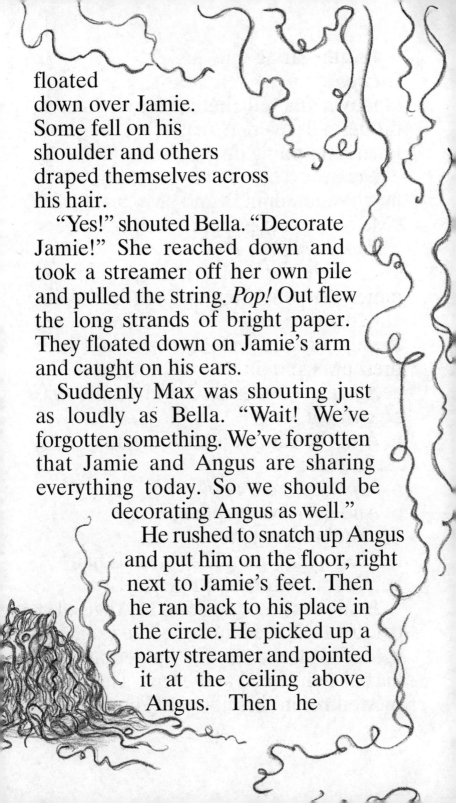

floated
down over Jamie.
Some fell on his
shoulder and others
draped themselves across
his hair.

"Yes!" shouted Bella. "Decorate Jamie!" She reached down and took a streamer off her own pile and pulled the string. *Pop!* Out flew the long strands of bright paper. They floated down on Jamie's arm and caught on his ears.

Suddenly Max was shouting just as loudly as Bella. "Wait! We've forgotten something. We've forgotten that Jamie and Angus are sharing everything today. So we should be decorating Angus as well."

He rushed to snatch up Angus and put him on the floor, right next to Jamie's feet. Then he ran back to his place in the circle. He picked up a party streamer and pointed it at the ceiling above Angus. Then he pulled the string.

Pop!

Down floated the coloured threads, falling all over Angus's stubby little horns and piling up on his hooves.

Now everyone began shouting "Go!" and "Watch mine!" and "My turn!" and "Me next!" and popping their streamers.

Pop! Pop! Pop! Pop!

The threads of brightly coloured paper kept shooting up high in the air, and drifting down all over Jamie and Angus, tangling in their hair and over their eyes and on their shoulders.

At first it was fun, and Jamie was enjoying it.

And then it got a bit too noisy and a bit too tangly.

Pop! Pop! Pop! Pop!

And everyone kept shouting.

"You missed that bit!"

"Try and get more on Jamie's hair!"

"Decorate them completely!"

Jamie took a peek down at Angus. He could hardly see him now. The rainbow-coloured streamers had landed all over his back and head and horns. They were twisted round his hooves. They draped all over his tail. Angus didn't look like a little Highland bull any more. He looked like a brightly-coloured *haystack*, and all Jamie could see of him was one small brown eye, peeping out nervously.

In fact, thought Jamie, the small brown eye looked really very worried indeed.

In fact, it looked *scared*.

41

Jamie made up his mind. "Right!" he shouted over all the noise. "That's enough! Everyone stop!"

He wasn't going to let Angus's share of the birthday be spoiled for him. And he could tell that all the shouting and popping and tangling was beginning to frighten poor Angus.

"It's somebody else's turn to be in the

middle," Jamie told all of them firmly. "Because this is my birthday and Angus's birthday, and we would like a little go at popping now, please."

He glanced down at Angus again, and thought the eye that he could see was looking a tiny bit happier.

"Can I be in the middle?" shouted Bella.

"And me!" called Max.

So Bella and Max went in the middle of the circle and they got popped and tangled. And then Tasha and Georgie had a turn at being decorated. And by the time they had run out of streamers, everyone at the party looked almost as much like a haystack as Angus.

After the last guest had gone, Jamie lay back on the rug with Angus tucked under his arm.

"That was *brilliant*!" he said. "The best party *ever*."

Jamie's father looked round at all the coloured streamers covering the floor and lamps and furniture and Jamie and Angus. "It's going to be *impossible* to clear this up," he grumbled. "Quite *impossible*."

"That's Edward for you," Jamie's mother said.

Jamie rolled over to pull a few of the tangly paper threads away from Angus's ear so he could whisper to him. "I know you didn't like the being-in-the-middle bit," he told him. "But you mustn't worry. Uncle Edward will bring us a different impossible present next time. And anyway, it will be a full twelve months until we have another birthday. That's a whole *year*."

And suddenly the one eye he could see under the tangles began to look a whole lot happier.

A NEW WAY TO CRY

Jamie staggered out of his bedroom with a pile of books. He carried them down to where Daddy was pulling the damp sheets out of the washing-machine.

Jamie dumped the books on the floor and picked up the first. It was called *The Sad and Lonely Bunny*. He opened it at the first page. There was a picture of a very unhappy rabbit with tears spurting out of his eyes onto the grass in front of him.

"My tears don't do that," Jamie complained to Daddy. "They don't go

flying away from me all over the grass."

"No," said his father. "I don't believe I've ever seen your tears do anything like that."

Jamie opened the next book at one of the nursery rhyme pages where Little Bo Peep was sitting hunched over with her hands covering her face.

"She's crying, isn't she?" He checked with Daddy. "Because she's lost her sheep."

"That's right," his father agreed. "She's crying."

"I don't cover my face with my hands like that when I'm crying," said Jamie.

"Neither do I," said Daddy. "But that's the way she does it."

Jamie rooted through the third book until he found the picture of a little boy about his own age wearing bright red knickerbockers. The boy had screwed up his face.

"And when you get to this bit in this story," Jamie reminded his father, "you always go 'Boohoo!'"

"I do," said Daddy. "Because that's what the words say." And he pointed. "Here. 'Boohoo! Boohoo!'"

"But," Jamie said triumphantly, "when we read *The Crosspatch Little Baby*, you say 'Waaaa-waaaa! Waaaa-waaaa!'." He turned the pages of *The Crosspatch Little Baby* until he found the right picture.

His father put down the laundry basket and ran his finger along a line of small letters swooping out of the crosspatch little baby's mouth and all the way across the picture. "Because that's what these letters say," he said to Jamie. "'Waaaa-waaaa! Waaaa-waaaa!'"

"Well," Jamie told him, "when I cry,

my tears don't jump out of my eyes onto the grass. And I don't cover my face with my hands. And I don't say boohoo. And I don't yell waaaa-waaaa. So maybe I'm not crying right."

"Nonsense," said Daddy. "There's no right way to cry. Everyone does it in their own way."

"Can I choose a new way to cry, then?" Jamie asked. "All by myself, with Angus."

"Probably," said his father. "Just make sure you don't charge into the pole of the whirligig clothes drier, like you did last week, and give yourself something to cry about."

Jamie sat under the damp sheets flapping round the pole of the whirligig drier in the garden and cuddled Angus while he thought about ways of crying.

Apart from crashing into the pole, the last time he'd cried was when Maria had hit him at nursery and Anthony had laughed, and he'd only let a few tears roll down his cheeks, and sniffed a bit. Mrs Bennett had pulled him onto her knee and cuddled him while she made Maria and Anthony say they were sorry. And then he'd felt better.

The time before that, he'd cried in the supermarket when Mummy made him get out of the trolley because he was being silly. But that was more of a tantrum really: he'd thrown himself on the floor and yelled until she pulled him to his feet and carried him outside, screaming and kicking, and gave him a serious ticking-off.

Then, as he'd behaved so badly, she wouldn't buy him the toy windmill that she'd practically promised him. He'd had

51

to wait ages before she'd gone to that shop again.

He'd cried when he trapped his finger in the cupboard door. But he couldn't remember much about that because it had hurt so much he only remembered the hurting, and having the plaster stuck on afterwards.

"I'm going to choose a new cry," he said to Angus. He set Angus down across from him, so he could watch. "And you can help me choose. You never cry, so you'll be a fair judge."

Angus sat waiting, paying a good deal of attention.

"Right," Jamie said. "I'm going to try and spurt some tears out now. All over the grass, like the sad and lonely bunny."

He screwed up his face and tried. But not one single tear would trickle out.

53

He tried for a long time. But it was hopeless.

"That didn't work," he told Angus. "So now I'm going to try the Little Bo Peep way."

Jamie covered his face with his hands, just like Bo Peep did in the picture. Nothing came out of his eyes. He didn't even find himself sobbing.

"That's a bit boring," he admitted to Angus. "And dark. I think I might skip that one and try boohooing instead."

Angus listened carefully as Jamie began to boohoo. Jamie enjoyed boohooing. He got louder and louder.

Suddenly the back door opened and Jamie's father came out carrying one last pillowcase he'd just found in the washing-machine. He poked his head in between the flapping sheets until he found Jamie and Angus.

"What *is* that dreadful noise?" he asked.

"What noise?" said Jamie.

"That noise like a cow with a bad tummy ache."

"Oh, *that*." Jamie shrugged. "That's just me, trying boohooing."

"Well, don't try it quite so loudly," his father warned. "Or Mrs Beadle will come round from next door to see what's wrong with you."

"I was about to stop anyway," said Jamie. "Angus and I are moving on to waaaa-waaaaing now."

For safety's sake, he waited until he heard the back door close before he started waaaa-waaaaing.

It went rather well. Jamie enjoyed it, and it was obvious that Angus was impressed.

"Waaaa-waaaa!   Waaaa-waaaa! Waaaa-waaaaaa!" He so enjoyed it that he carried on, over and over, and getting louder and louder.

Finally he stopped, and turned to Angus. "That's the best," he said. And Angus looked as if he probably agreed.

Just then, they heard next door's gate creak, and then their own gate squeak, and footsteps crunching on the gravel path. There were a lot of little thuds, as if someone was running very fast across the grass towards them. They heard Mrs Beadle's voice calling, "Jamie? Jamie? Are you all right, dear?"

Then suddenly they heard her trip. There was a cry of "Whooah!" as Mrs Beadle bumped into the whirligig's pole and fell, all wrapped in sheets, knocking the pole down and tangling Jamie and Angus up so hard in washing that it made Jamie cry in a new way.

"Yeeeeow! Yeeeeow! *Yeeeeow!*"

It took Jamie's father quite a while to untangle everyone. Mrs Beadle was fine. She went off home, and Jamie came indoors to get his face washed after all the tears.

"What noise did I make?" he asked his father when they were sitting together at the table afterwards, having a quiet time to calm down after all the excitement.

"'Yeeeeow!'" said Daddy. "Very loud. And very often. For quite a long time."

"I must be a yeeeeower, then," Jamie told Daddy ruefully. "Angus and I had only just chosen that I'd be a waaaaer. But I don't think how you cry is something that you get to choose. I think I'm stuck with yeeeeow."

He thought back to all the sheets tangling around him and pulling him this way and that as the pole fell, and how much it had hurt when his head banged on the hard ground.

"*And* you don't get to choose what you cry about," he added sadly.

"No," Daddy said. "You certainly don't get to choose what you cry about. But never mind. If you're lucky, you get to choose a few things. Like what you want to do. And who you want to do it with."

"I suppose I'm lucky then," said Jamie. "Because I know what I want to do. And I know who I want to do it with."

And, sliding off his chair, he gave his daddy a big hug and a kiss, and went off to his bedroom to play shipwrecks with Angus.

THE EATING SLOWLY RACE

Jamie was eating his pudding. He was eating it as fast as he could so that he and Angus could get back down under the table and finish the game they were playing.

"Stop gobbling!" his mother said sternly. "Take sensible spoonfuls. And keep your mouth closed till you've finished swallowing. Half-chewed food swirling around in your mouth looks absolutely disgusting."

Jamie chewed and swallowed carefully. Then he opened his mouth to complain. "First I'm told to eat faster,

59

and then I'm told to eat slower."

Curious, his father asked him, "Who tells you to eat faster?"

"Uncle Edward," answered Jamie. "When you go out and he comes round to look after me, we always have an eating fast race."

"Oh, do you?" said Daddy, and he gave Jamie's mother one of his "Your brother!" looks.

"And Uncle Edward always wins," admitted Jamie sourly. "That's why he keeps on telling me to eat faster—so that the race will be more fun for him."

"Of course he always wins," said

Jamie's mother. "He has a bigger mouth."

"*Too* big," said Daddy. But Mummy gave him one of her "Be careful what you say" looks before she turned to Jamie.

"Well, I have a good idea. Next time Uncle Edward comes round to babysit, and you have supper together, you tell him that the name of the game has changed, and now it's the eating slowly race."

"All right." Jamie nodded. "And I'll make sure that Angus is allowed to be in the race as well, because he never actually swallows anything I put on his plate. So even if Uncle Edward and I are slow as snails, Angus will still win."

He grinned at Angus, and Angus couldn't help looking pleased. He wasn't used to winning any of the games or races or competitions he did with Jamie unless Jamie let him, so this would make a nice change.

"That's settled, then," said Mummy. "But while you're having supper with us, we don't want you eating fast and we don't want you eating slowly. Just *sensible* eating with Daddy and me, please."

"All right," agreed Jamie, and he picked up his spoon and went back to his pudding.

Next time Uncle Edward came round to babysit, Jamie told him the rules had changed.

"It's an eating slowly race now."

"Oh, is it?" said Uncle Edward. "And why is that, then?"

"Because Mummy says gobbling is disgusting," said Jamie. "And Granny always says that people who open their mouths to shove in more food while the last lot is still going round look like cement mixers."

Uncle Edward sighed. "Good job there's plenty of salad tonight," he said. "Because if it's an eating slowly race, the food is going to get very cold."

"You could eat your baked potato while it's still hot," Jamie suggested cunningly. "And, just this once, lose the race."

"No thanks," said Uncle Edward. "I hate losing. If I can win all our eating fast races, I can win this race too."

"We'll see," said Jamie. He gave Angus a little secret look and was quite sure that Angus gave him one back.

Uncle Edward set out the supper on the plates. Both of them had a baked potato, a slice of spinach and onion tart, two spoonfuls of peas and some salad.

"What about Angus?" Jamie reminded his uncle.

"Whoops!" Uncle Edward said. "I always forget that Angus likes to have his supper too." And he found a third plate and gave Angus a tiny lump of potato, a shred of lettuce, one pea and the smallest dab of tart ever seen.

"Happy?" Uncle Edward asked Angus. And certainly Angus looked quite content, so Uncle Edward and Jamie started their eating slowly race.

First Jamie took a tiny bite of baked potato and chewed it well.

Uncle Edward did the same.

Jamie took another bite and chewed it even more thoroughly.

So did Uncle Edward.

Jamie lifted his fork for the third time.

"This is so *boring*," Uncle Edward grumbled. "And everything's getting cold. Why don't we gobble up our baked potato, then start the race over again?"

"All right," said Jamie. "But no gobbling,

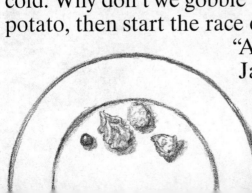

because I'm not allowed to gobble."

So both of them ate up their baked potato while they chatted about how stupid flies are when they're trying to get out of a window.

Then Uncle Edward cut off a tiny sliver of his spinach and onion tart and chewed it well.

Jamie did exactly the same.

Uncle Edward took another, even slimmer, sliver of tart and chewed it even more slowly.

So did Jamie.

Uncle Edward stuck his knife into his slice of tart for the third time.

"This is so *boring*," Jamie complained. "And it only

tastes good in proper mouthfuls. Why don't we finish up our tart, then start the race over again with the peas and the lettuce?"

"Good plan," said Uncle Edward.

So they ate the tart while they chatted about Uncle Edward's new girlfriend's disgusting and bad-tempered spitting cat.

"Right," Uncle Edward announced. "Back to the race!"

He stabbed a pea with his fork and chewed it thoroughly.

So did Jamie.

Uncle Edward took a second pea.

So did Jamie.

"This is so *boring*," Uncle Edward moaned. "Why don't we both eat all our peas except for the last five, then start the race again?"

"Fine by me," Jamie told him.

They each ate all their peas except for the last five, then went back to the race.

"This is so *boring*," Jamie said. "Why don't we eat all the salad except for one last tiny leaf, then start the race again?"

"Done!" Uncle Edward agreed.

So they did that.

"Right," Uncle Edward said. "Now that I'm nowhere near as hungry as I was before, I'm going to win this race."

He took about five whole minutes to put one pea in his mouth. When he had finished chewing it, he said, "I've got an idea. Why don't you eat one pea to even up with me, and then we can get down from the table and play snap for a few minutes?"

68

"OK," said Jamie. "You find the cards and I'll sit here and eat my pea."

So Uncle Edward went off to find the cards and shuffle them while Jamie ate his pea. While he was chewing, Jamie peeped over his shoulder to make sure Uncle Edward wasn't looking, then quickly slid one of his four leftover peas under his shred of lettuce where it couldn't be seen and where somebody sitting across the table might even forget all about it. Then he left Angus staring at his own plate, and got down to play cards.

They played for about half an hour, then went back to the table.

"Your turn!" said Jamie quickly.

So Uncle Edward ate a second pea.

"Your turn now!" said Uncle Edward, so Jamie ate a second pea too.

"Your turn," said Jamie, and Uncle Edward ate a third pea.

"Your turn," said Uncle Edward, and Jamie ate a third pea.

"Your turn," said Jamie, and Uncle Edward ate his fourth pea.

"Your turn," said Uncle Edward, and Jamie ate the only pea Uncle Edward could see on his plate because Jamie's last pea was still hidden under the lettuce.

"My turn," said Uncle Edward, and he ate his last pea. "Now shall we have a quick game of dominoes before we start on the lettuce?"

"Yes, please," said Jamie.

So they got out the dominoes and played for quite a while, until they remembered the eating slowly race.

Uncle Edward glanced at his watch. "Your mum and dad will be home soon," he warned Jamie. "So, as boring as this eating slowly race is, we had better get on and finish it, because I really want to win."

"OK," agreed Jamie.

They went back to the table. They each cut tiny, tiny, tiny slivers off their last shred of lettuce and chewed them slowly till they both had just one tiny sliver of a shred of lettuce left.

"This is so boring I can't stand it," Uncle Edward finally admitted. "Let's make a deal. We'll both stab our forks into our last shreds of lettuce and eat them together and call it a fair draw."

Jamie said nothing, but he stabbed his last shred of lettuce (very, very carefully) with his fork.

"One, two, three—go!" shouted Uncle Edward.

Keeping their eyes locked on to one another to make sure there was no cheating, both of them lifted their forks and swallowed their last shred of lettuce.

"Draw!" Uncle Edward announced.

"No," Jamie corrected him. He pointed to the one last lonely pea that he'd been hiding under his lettuce. "This time I beat you."

Uncle Edward laughed. "Well, well," he said. "The winner!"

"Not the *real* winner," Jamie told him, and he pointed to Angus's plate on which there still sat a tiny lump of potato, a shred of lettuce, one pea and the smallest dab of tart ever seen.

"I didn't know Angus was in the race with us," said Uncle Edward.

"Of course he was in the race with us," said Jamie. "Angus and I do everything together. You know that."

"I suppose I do," said Uncle Edward. "All right, then. Angus is the real winner." He turned to Angus. "Congratulations!" he told him. "Jolly well done. A brilliant performance and an excellent win! Good on you, Angus!"

And though Angus was bowing his head very

72

modestly in front of his winning plate, Jamie and Uncle Edward could easily tell that he was thrilled to bits to have the unusual treat of being the real winner.

JAMIE THE GENIUS

Jamie was sitting in the bath, making his ducks swim in a circle and telling his mother about his day at nursery.

"Mrs Bennett called me a genius."

His mother smiled. "Did she?"

"Yes," Jamie said. "She did."

He made his ducks swim round the other way and asked his mother, "So what's a genius?"

"A very clever person," Mummy told him. "And you are certainly that."

"I am," said Jamie. "I was the only person who could think of a way to get Bella's balloon down from the ceiling."

"The nursery ceiling is really high," his mother said. "If it was one of those balloons that floats up by itself, I don't see how anyone could ever have got it down again."

"I thought of a way," said Jamie. "All by myself." And he lined up his ducks in a row so they could listen while he told his mother exactly how they'd done it.

"First we borrowed another floaty balloon from Max and I told Mrs Bennett to tie it on a longer string. Much longer. Then I said she should press sticky tape on top of Max's balloon, and make sure some of the tacky bit was sticking up."

He made a fist and plonked it on his

head. "Like this. Like a little sticky-tape hat on the top of the balloon."

"This is *amazing*," said his mother. "What then?"

Jamie made sure that all his ducks were back in line and listening properly before he went on with his story.

"Then Mrs Bennett stood under Bella's lost balloon and let Max's balloon float up and up on the end of its very long string. And when it got up there, the sticky-tape hat bit couldn't help sort of kissing Bella's balloon and getting stuck to it."

He put one fist on top of the other to show his mother how Max's balloon had stuck itself to Bella's.

"And then Mrs Bennett pulled the string—very, very gently—and both the balloons came down together."

"My golly!" said his mother. "Mrs Bennett's right. You *are* a genius."

"Yes." Jamie nodded. "I think I

76

might be. It was very clever. And Bella was so happy she said I could look after her pet gerbil for three whole days while she goes on a trip with her family."

"Oh, yes?" said Jamie's mother. "And what did you say when she told you that?"

Jamie replied very happily, "I said yes!"

His mother sighed. "Now that," she said with feeling, "was maybe not *quite* so clever."

The gerbil was called Lulu. Bella's dad

brought her round in her cage and asked, "Where shall I put it?"

"In *my* room," insisted Jamie. "Angus and I want Lulu to stay with us."

Angus didn't look too sure, but he didn't say anything.

"You won't be able to play shipwrecks," Mummy warned. "In case you make a mistake and fall on the cage."

"That's all right," Jamie said. "Angus and I can manage for a whole weekend without playing shipwrecks."

He glanced at Angus. Angus didn't look too pleased. But then again, he didn't look all that cross either.

"And you won't be able to do roly-

polies across the floor," Mummy added. "In case you knock the cage over."

"All right," agreed Jamie. "No roly-polies."

He glanced at Angus again. Angus 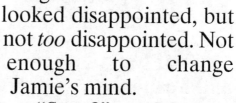 looked disappointed, but not *too* disappointed. Not enough to change Jamie's mind.

"Sure?" Mummy asked him.

"Sure," Jamie said.

So Lulu's cage was put in Jamie's room. Jamie had never had a pet before, so he spent almost all day watching Lulu running inside the little wheel that creaked as it went round, and rooting about in her bedding. From time to time he took her out of the cage and let her walk up one arm, over his shoulders, and down

79

the other arm, while Angus looked on, clearly a little bored.

"Try to make friends," Jamie encouraged him. And he held Lulu close up to Angus's nose so they could meet each other.

Before he could stop her, Lulu had fixed her sharp little teeth into Angus's snout and bitten him. Hard. Jamie was horrified. He put Lulu back in her cage and comforted poor Angus. "Never mind," he kept on telling him. "It's only for three days. Bella will be back on Sunday."

At bedtime, Jamie checked Lulu still had plenty of water in her bottle and food in her tray. Then he washed his hands very thoroughly indeed, cleaned his teeth and got into bed with Angus beside him on

80

the pillow. It was Mummy's turn to read a story and kiss them and turn off the light.

And then the creaking started.

Creak, creak. Creak, creak.

Creak, creak, creak, creak.

Jamie sat up and switched on the bedside light.

Lulu was running in her little wheel.

"Sssh!" Jamie told her. "Angus and I are trying to get to sleep. Go to bed, Lulu."

But Lulu wouldn't.

She just kept running in the wheel. *Creak, creak, creak, creak.* Jamie tried pulling the covers over his head, but he could still hear it.

It took poor Jamie ages to get to sleep, and in the morning he felt tired and crabby.

So did Angus.

Next evening, Daddy took the wheel out of the cage and put it down on the other side of the bars.

"Goodnight, Jamie," he said.

"Goodnight, Angus. And goodnight to you too, Lulu. Try to be a little quieter."

But Lulu wouldn't. Jamie was just on the verge of falling asleep when the

scrabbling started.

Scrabble, scrabble.

Scrabble, scrabble.

Scrabble, scrabble,

scrabble, scrabble.

Jamie sat up and switched on the light. Lulu was trying to get to her wheel through the bars of the cage.

"Oh, no!" wailed Jamie. He pulled the

covers over his head again. *Scrabble, scrabble, scrabble, scrabble.* That night, it took even longer to get to sleep, and Jamie and Angus were even more crabby in the morning.

On the last evening, Jamie's mother didn't just take the wheel out of the cage. She hid it behind a bookshelf.

"Now she won't scratch to get at it," Mummy said. "So things will be quieter."

They weren't, though. Jamie and Angus had only just begun to fall asleep when the noise started.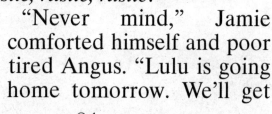

Rustle, rustle. Rustle, rustle.

Rustle, rustle, rustle, rustle.

Jamie sat up and switched on the light so that he and Angus could see what the problem was this time. Lulu was mucking about in her nest. *Rustle, rustle, rustle, rustle.*

"Never mind," Jamie comforted himself and poor tired Angus. "Lulu is going home tomorrow. We'll get

84

some peace and quiet then."

Early next evening, Bella and her father came to pick up Lulu.

Bella held Lulu close to Jamie's face. "Do you want to kiss her goodbye?"

"Not really, no," said Jamie. "We did all that goodbye stuff earlier, before you came."

Bella bent down to Angus. "What about you?" And without even waiting to see what Angus wanted, she pushed Lulu forward, close to his snout. Jamie reached out to snatch Angus to safety in case Lulu bit his nose again, and Bella was so startled she stopped holding Lulu properly.

Lulu wriggled out of Bella's hands and leaped onto the sofa. Without even pausing to look round, she scuttled over the cushions and dropped down to the rug.

Then, before anyone could stop her, she vanished under the sofa.

Bella's father looked at his watch. "Oh, bother! We're in a hurry and it takes ages to coax her out from under the furniture. So can we leave Lulu with you for one more night?"

Angus looked very nervous suddenly.

"Surely there's something we can do!" said Jamie's mother. "Tip up the sofa, perhaps?"

Bella's father shook his head. "She might be sitting at the back and get squashed. Or rush out and hide somewhere else."

But Jamie's mother wasn't giving up. "Then we'll block all around the bottom of the sofa with cushions, and only leave her one small place to come out—straight through the door into her cage."

Bella's father shook his head again. "If

she's not hungry, then that could take hours."

"Oh dear!" said Jamie's mother.

Jamie gave Angus a little sideways peek, and Angus gave Jamie one back. Angus was looking really worried now, Jamie thought, as if he feared that at any moment Lulu might rush out from under the sofa and bite him on the snout again.

Jamie knew it was up to him. If he could rescue Bella's balloon at nursery, then surely he could rescue Angus too.

Jamie took charge.

"I've got a plan," he said. "Put all the cushions around the bottom of the sofa, just like Mummy said."

Everyone obediently jammed cushions around the bottom of the sofa, except for one little hole just big enough for a gerbil to squeeze through.

"Now put the cage next to the hole, with the door open so Lulu can run in," said Jamie.

Bella did that.

"Now," Jamie announced. "We need the hairdryer."

So Daddy went off to fetch that, and plugged it in behind the sofa.

"Set it to full," ordered Jamie. "So the air comes out in a real whoosh. And set it to cold as well."

Mummy set it to full and cold.

"Now poke it between the cushions we put down to stop Lulu getting out at this end," said Jamie.

They all watched as Mummy kneeled

on the floor at one end of the sofa and
Bella stood ready by the cage at the
other.

"Now *blow!*" said Jamie.

Mummy turned on the hairdryer, and
everyone heard the giant WHOOSH of
cold air blasting under the sofa.

They didn't have to wait long. Almost
at once there was a little squeak of
disgust, a scrabble of tiny feet, and out
of the hole at the other end and into the
cage shot little Lulu, running very fast.

Quickly she buried herself inside her warm nest and didn't even poke out her nose again until Bella had slammed the cage door and fastened the catch.

"There!" Jamie said. "Now Lulu can go home tonight!"

"Goody!" said Bella.

"Goody!" said Jamie's mother.

"Goody!" said Jamie.

And you could tell that if he had been going to say anything at all, Angus would definitely have said "Goody!" too.

Later, when Jamie was in the bath, making his ducks swim in a circle, his mother said, "That was the cleverest idea ever. Mrs Bennett is right. You *are* a genius, Jamie."

"It *was* a good idea, wasn't it?" Jamie agreed. He looked up at Angus, who was sitting safely and comfortably on the warm towel rail. "But I had to think of something to save poor Angus."

"So you did," said his mother. "Angus is lucky to have such a good friend in you."

"And I am lucky to have such a good friend in him," said Jamie. "I think that probably we might be best friends for ever."

"Yes," Jamie's mother agreed. "I think you might."

And up on the towel rail, Angus looked as if he thought that he and Jamie might be best friends for ever too.